Santa Gets a Second Job

MICHELE D'IGNAZIO

Illustrated by Sergio Olivotti

Translated by Denise Muir

MACMILLAN CHILDREN'S BOOKS

First published in Italy as *Il Secondo Lavoro di Babbo Natale*
© 2019 Mondadori Libri S.p.A., Milano under the imprint RIZZOLI

This English language edition published 2020 by Macmillan Children's Books
an imprint of Pan Macmillan
The Smithson, 6 Briset Street, London EC1M 5NR
Associated companies throughout the world
www.panmacmillan.com

ISBN 978-1-5290-5152-0

Text by Michele D'Ignazio
Illustrations by Sergio Olivotti
Translation copyright © Denise Muir 2020

All rights reserved. No part of this publication may be reproduced,
stored in a retrieval system, or transmitted, in any form or by any means
(electronic, mechanical, photocopying, recording or otherwise),
without the prior written permission of the publisher.

Pan Macmillan does not have any control over, or any responsibility for,
any author or third-party websites referred to in or on this book.

1 3 5 7 9 8 6 4 2

A CIP catalogue record for this book is available from the British Library.

Printed and bound in Poland by Dimograf

This book is sold subject to the condition that it shall not,
by way of trade or otherwise, be lent, resold, hired out,
or otherwise circulated without the publisher's prior consent
in any form of binding or cover other than that in which
it is published and without a similar condition including this
condition being imposed on the subsequent purchaser.

A tutti quelli che ancora scrivono lettere

To all those who still write letters

1

Santa Claus was a seasonal worker, employed once a year over the very busy Christmas period. As you can imagine, delivering presents to all the children in the world was an important job and extremely exhausting. But it also meant he could go into slipper mode and take a break for the rest of the year. From January to November, Santa Claus was on holiday.

And Santa certainly enjoyed being on holiday!

When he was young, he'd always hoped to find the kind of job that would give him a lot (seriously, a lot) of spare time.

So, what did he do for the rest of the year?

Well, he read books, watched television, played cards with his friends, took the reindeer for walks. He was an excellent cook and made delicious dinners.

He also renewed his gym membership every

year, thinking he might get fit, but somehow it never quite worked out.

All in all, Santa Claus was a bit of a lazybones. He enjoyed the easy life.

2

Unfortunately, times had changed.

The International Postal Service was in the red. That doesn't mean the workers all dressed in red like Santa, it meant that the Postal Service had run out of money. It was worse than just having no money, though. The Postal Service also owed lots of money to lots of people and, for three years now, Santa Claus hadn't been paid for the important home-delivery service he provided. He was a good old age by this point, but retirement wasn't an option and he loved his job.

The hard times continued, and this year the

International Postal Service announced that it would no longer be taking on new staff.

Every year, thousands of aspiring young Santa Clauses would arrive at the Postal Service's employment office, creating the most enormous

queue all the way round the imposing building.

They didn't need to bring a CV with them. There were only three requirements to get a job as a Santa's helper:

1. Have a long beard

2. Look jolly

The next one was the most important, the reason most aspiring Santas were rejected . . .

3. Be kind and generous

Truly kind and generous. Not sort of, not pretending to be, but properly, actually kind.

It was easy to check the first two requirements. The Super Director of the Postal Service just had to look at the applicant. The third one was a bit trickier.

3

It has to be said that the most unkind and ungenerous of all was the International Postal Service itself.

The Super Director never gave the younger workers a permanent contract. The most they could hope for was temporary work as Santa's helpers on Christmas Eve.

This caused an even bigger problem. It meant that Santa had to work with new, inexperienced helpers every year and he never got the chance to teach them the job properly.

And what a lot of trouble the helpers caused.

They'd send the parcels to all the wrong people, causing floods of tears and uncontrollable hiccupping from children on Christmas morning.

Some, having only recently passed their driving test, would make a mess of steering the reindeer. They'd get tangled up in tree branches and snared in overhead power lines, which was also very dangerous.

Sometimes, they'd veer too quickly to the right or left, and parcels would tumble out of the sleigh.

For two years in a row, live images had been broadcast around the world of the surprise (and, for the International Postal Service, rather embarrassing) phenomenon of parcel-shaped hail storms.

So, despite having lots of helpers over the years, Santa Claus had ended up doing most of the work himself. And this year, he would have no help at all.

These were lean times indeed, and lean times were not really Santa's cup of tea.

4

To make matters worse, there was the problem of reindeer hire. Santa Claus only had two reindeer of his own – Dasher and Dancer – who lived in his garage.

He needed more than a hundred reindeer to do his job, so had to hire the rest.

Hire charges were rising and the price of carrots was going up every year. And, as if that wasn't bad enough, the few days they were on duty, the reindeer ate enough to feed a reindeer army.

Then there was sleigh insurance, sleigh tax, sleigh washing and hoof maintenance. Santa Claus paid a team of experts for these services and had invested in more than one hundred pairs of slippers to keep the reindeers' hooves warm when they were resting.

But, with no money for maintenance, all sorts of things could go wrong.

Sometimes Santa Claus would have nightmares and wake up in a sweat about the dramatic front-page headlines he'd dreamt about:

SLEIGH PLUMMETS FROM SKY! OLD MAN SURVIVES, BUT CHILDREN'S GIFTS ALL LOST.

How could the situation have become so bad?

The answer lay in the children's letters to Santa. Once upon a time, they had only made one or two small requests that could be delivered easily. Usually, all it took was a simple gift made with love – a small homemade toy or a bag of sweets. Recently, however, the letters were more like never-ending lists and the constant requests had pushed the International Postal Service over the edge and into the red.

5

It was November and Christmas would soon be here.

Santa Claus was normally a very cheerful, optimistic person, but recently he'd been feeling a bit miserable. It wasn't like him.

He was having a recurring nightmare that he'd been replaced by a robot. Or, worse still, by an army of remote-controlled drones operated by a computer.

He'd wake up shaking.

'Drones delivering presents?' he muttered to himself indignantly. 'Delivering presents is not a

mission for the military! There will always be room for Santa and his sleigh.'

But he was in for a big surprise.

The Super Director of the International Postal Service made the announcement on the news.

'We need to lower costs and, more importantly,

we need faster deliveries and more streamlined requests. So no more letters! We'll only be taking bullet-pointed wish lists from smartphones from now on.'

Santa Claus nearly fell off his chair.

'No, this can't be happening!' he cried, getting

angrier by the minute. 'This . . . this means there'll be no more "Dear Santa", "Happy Christmas", "Best Wishes" and "I love you". In their letters, children tell me all about their families, their friends and their favourite things. They ask me about the reindeer . . . Now all that is going to disappear!'

Santa Claus had gone pale.

He *loved* the children's letters. They were always full of happiness, hope and excitement. The very special ones were stored in a box under his bed and he liked to take them out and re-read them during his eleven-month holiday.

'I'll write a letter of protest!' he exclaimed.

But it was Santa who received a letter that day. Opening it, he saw it had been typed on a computer and signed (in very messy handwriting) in the bottom left by the Super Director of the Postal Service. Santa scanned the few lines quickly. He couldn't breathe. His heart lurched.

It was a letter of dismissal.

He'd been sacked!

6

'After all these years of loyal service, I've lost my job!' Santa grumbled from behind his long white beard.

He hadn't seen this coming at all!

But Santa Claus couldn't stay down for long. After all, how could the International Postal Service manage without him? How would the children get their Christmas presents? It must be a terrible mistake. Christmas wouldn't be Christmas without Santa Claus.

In the meantime, action was needed.

Santa rushed out to the garage, still wearing his

red pyjamas and slippers, got the reindeer ready and zoomed over to the nearby newsagent's to buy a newspaper. He flicked past the front pages and the international news. What he was looking for was at the back – the job ads.

'Mr Claus, you should have your hat on – it's cold out today' the newsagent said.

On his way home, Santa Claus noticed a barber's shop. He'd been thinking of trimming his long beard for years, but

had never been able to pluck up enough courage.
Perhaps now was the time . . .

He pulled the reindeer over and peered into the
place that had always been so mystifying to him.
From where he was standing outside, he could

hear the snip-snip of the barber's scissors and the niggling noise of the electric clippers.

Santa Claus gave a heavy sigh then went on his way, urging the reindeer to fly as fast as they could.

Sitting comfortably in his armchair later that evening, Santa Claus was feeling fairly cheerful. In his many years on the job, he'd overcome every kind of complication: wrong addresses, children catching him red-handed delivering presents, dogs biting his bottom, chimneys and windows too narrow to get through, alarms going off. One night, he'd even had a security guard shine a torch in his face.

'Who's there? Who are you?'

'How can you not recognize me? Can I just get on with my work, please? I still have ten million

three hundred and forty-seven thousand and twenty-three deliveries to make!' Santa Claus had grumbled in reply.

With all these mishaps in mind, he browsed the ads in the hope he'd soon find the right job to tide him over.

The first one that caught his eye was this:

> City-centre restaurant seeks dynamic, well-presented waiter, willing to work late at night. Send CV and photo.

Santa's first thought on reading it was that he'd probably make a better chef, than a waiter. A kitchen full of steaming pots and pans was his favourite place to be. And as a chef he'd have to taste everything he cooked. Yes, it would definitely be the perfect job for him.

Unfortunately there were no adverts for chefs, so he went back to the original vacancy. He read it again. 'Send CV and photo'. How would he do that?

'By email', it said.

'But I don't have a computer!' Santa thought a bit more about it. 'I'm sure I must be fairly recognizable. I won't need a photo or CV. I'll just turn up in person.'

So off he went. He dragged the reindeer out of the garage again and pointed them in the direction of the city centre.

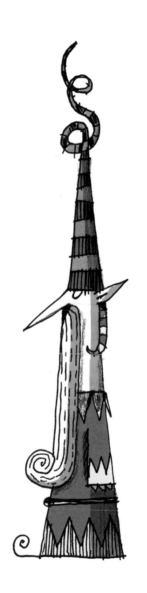

7

The restaurant owner's eyes nearly popped out when he saw Santa Claus walk in.

'Mr Claus!'

He *had* recognized him.

It won't be that hard, after all, getting a second job, Santa Claus thought to himself, confident he'd be promoted straight away to head chef.

'Please, let me show you to the best table in the house! Our chef has made the most delicious lasagne today.'

'What's this about a table? And lasagne? I'm here about the job!'

'What job?'

'The one in the paper.' Santa pulled out the newspaper with the job ad at the bottom, circled in thick blue pen.

The owner of the restaurant looked at Santa, baffled.

'Ha, ha, you're joking, aren't you? You already have a job!'

Santa Claus blushed. He didn't want to admit he'd been fired. Trying to play it cool, he said, 'Yes, but I'm looking for some extra hours.

I'm renovating the house, you see.'

An innocent little white lie, just like his beard.

But the restaurant owner's face had turned pale.
He hadn't been expecting Santa to say that. He
scratched his head, thought quickly about it then

braced himself. 'I'm honoured you'd like to apply, but . . .'

'But what?'

'But, well, the advert said we're looking for someone dynamic and well-presented.'

Santa Claus burst into a long, hearty laugh.

'I know it doesn't look it, but I can be very dynamic when I want to be.'

'I understand. But it's only a small restaurant – there's not much room between the tables – and you're . . .'

Santa Claus didn't wait for him to finish.

'I might be old but I'm very agile!' he insisted.

'Well, we'd rather that the people working for us have, well, that they have a clean face.'

'What are you suggesting? That I'm dirty? What do you take me for?'

'Yes, I know – but by clean, I meant without so

much hair on your face . . . It might dip into the customers' spaghetti, you see.'

'No!' Santa exclaimed, remembering the barber shop with a shudder. 'Not my beard!'

He turned on his heels and marched out of the restaurant, patting his beard as he left in a sort of *don't worry* kind of way.

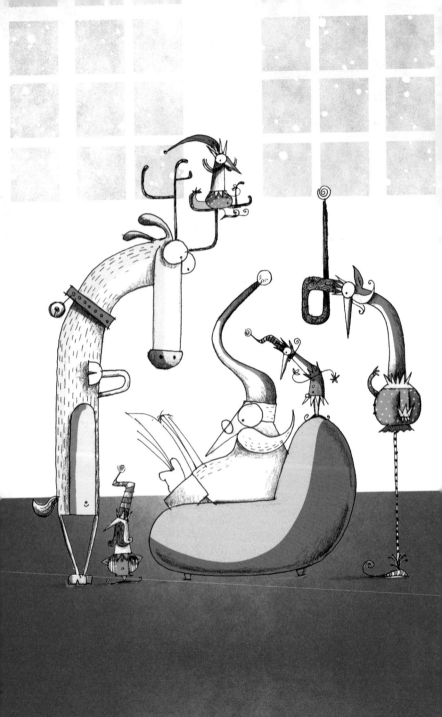

8

Santa muttered to himself all the way home. As soon as he got inside, he took out the newspaper and scanned the job ads again.

Party Planet seeks entertainer
for children's parties.
Requirements: lookalike to any famous
TV celebrity, good dancer and performer,
strong stage presence.

Santa puffed out his chest.

'Well, would you look at that? I'll give them TV celebrity! Children love me. And I know how to make them laugh – I don't need anyone telling me how to do that.'

He got the reindeer out and zoomed off to Party Planet.

9

Santa's house was miles away from everything, in case you didn't know, on the furthest outskirts of the city, where the fields turned to mountains and it snowed nearly all the time.

He wasn't aware he had a neighbour, but there was actually another little house not too far from his, about one hundred metres away, hidden where you could hardly see it. It's where Bea lived.

Bea had written lots of letters to Santa, possibly hundreds, over the years. She'd started when she was a child and still wrote them even now she was much, much older.

Her letters were a bit silly, full of strange questions and odd requests. They were also full of love and happiness, just as letters to Santa should be.

But, before we go any further, you need to know about the cauldron.

Each year, before the Christmas presents are wrapped and ready to deliver, the children's letters to Santa are all examined by an important and very bureaucratic department where a ruthless selection process takes place.

The much-feared selection staff only forward letters with requests for 'proper' presents.

Requests for anything 'abstract' follow a different procedure.

A small number make it through, nevertheless, thanks to the hard work and inventiveness of the workers at the International Postal Service.

All the other letters are thrown into the cauldron, an enormous ten-metre high, seven-metre wide, imagination-munching paper shredder, which turns children's wildest dreams into soggy confetti.

The letters most likely to end up in the cauldron tended to ask:

★ for world peace (thousands request this)
★ to be able to fly or become invisible
★ to be able to travel through time

The list got longer every year and the pile of letters waiting to be turned into confetti was bigger than anything you can imagine. At the time of this story, there were letters dating back years and years on the pile.

Under the Super Director's management, even more letters were ending up on the cauldron pile. He'd introduced a new rule and insisted it was rigorously applied: only requests for material goods would be processed.

As a result, none of Bea's letters had ever made it through the selection stage. They were rejected straight away and stamped F01 and F02: fanciful and impossible to fulfil. Her wishes always went ungranted, but she'd kept writing to Santa Claus all the same.

So what had Bea written in all those letters she'd sent to Santa?

She'd started a long time ago when she was just four years old:

Dear Santa Claus, you have
the best job in the world!
I think you're amazing!

She'd kept writing year after year, always showering Santa with compliments and never asking for anything:

You're such a wonderful person. I adore you. You seem like such good fun. I saw you on the television the other night. And in a film at the cinema. You might not have been in the lead role but you were so good . . .

And . . .

> **Dear Santa Claus,**
>
> **I know you're really busy, especially**
>
> **in winter, but I'd love to meet you.**
>
> **Do you think we could arrange it?**
>
> **Summer would be great!**

If Santa had been able to read all the letters, no doubt he would've blushed. But, of course, Bea's letters had all been added to the Postal Service's cauldron for being too fanciful. None of Bea's letters had ever made it through the selection stage.

In the meantime, she'd also moved to live in a little house, far, far away on a snowy plain.

There was only one other house in the vicinity, a hundred or so metres away, with a long chimney that had smoke puffing out of it all day long.

Oh, someone else likes to live remotely, just like me! I wonder who it can be? Bea had thought when she first saw the house . . .

10

You must be wondering how Santa's interview went at Party Planet.

Santa Claus strode inside, full of confidence, even though the restaurant fiasco had dented his pride just a little, if he was being honest.

The place was run by a young lady with blue-rimmed glasses, who looked a little surprised when Santa walked in. 'Are you here to pick someone up?' she asked. 'Are you a grandad?'

'Well no, actually . . .'

'Oh, I see, you'd like to register a grandchild, then? If so, you've come to the right place. We run activities in the morning and afternoon, and offer courses in cooking, gardening, drawing, theatre, dance—'

'That's not—' Santa Claus interrupted.

'Your grandchildren won't have time to be bored. This is the perfect place to park your little ones—'

'Well, actually . . .'

'Is there something wrong?'

The lady hadn't recognized him.

Santa had to admit he hadn't been on the television as much lately. People didn't seem to be so interested in Christmas cheer these days. But how could the woman not know who he was?

'You're not a tax collector, are you? Or the postman?'

'A postman? Well, I suppose you could say—' Santa Claus replied.

'What kind of uniform is that?'

'It's my suit. Anyway, I'm here about the job. I'm Santa Claus – children love me.'

'About the job?' the young woman asked, giggling.

'What's so funny?'

'I'm so sorry. I didn't mean to . . . but I think I should be straight with you and not waste your time. You don't fit any of our requirements – I'm sorry. The ad requested applicants aged eighteen to thirty.'

'Eighteen to thirty? Really? I never read that.'

'Could it be your eyesight, perhaps?'

'I can see perfectly well, thank you!'

'How old are you?'

'Well, I'm not really sure. I've lost count of the

years. Definitely more than thirty . . .'

'I'm so sorry. Goodbye.'

'But . . . can't you give me . . .'

The young woman stopped to think. 'Well, I could give you some hours in the cloakroom, looking after the children's coats. But I have to warn you, it doesn't pay a lot.'

Santa Claus left without saying goodbye.

To add insult to injury, when he got outside a traffic warden was hanging a parking fine on one of Dasher's horns.

'What are you doing? I've only been gone five minutes and I'm just leaving.'

'I'm sorry, this is a no-parking zone.'

Huffing and puffing, Santa stuffed the fine into his pocket and flew off home at top speed.

11

Bea had only recently learned who her odd neighbour was.

It had happened one very sunny afternoon a few weeks ago. She couldn't contain her curiosity any longer and had ventured all the way over to the solitary snow-bound house.

It was the very last one before the world turned into a gigantic sheet of ice.

The minute she saw the garage her suspicions were aroused: there was no car inside, only two reindeer and two massive piles of carrots.

Smoke puffed out of the chimney in a constant

stream and she could hear music coming from inside. It wasn't gentle, relaxing music, though. It was rock. She thought she could make out . . . Yes! It was a heavy-metal version of 'Jingle Bells'!

The noise had startled Bea, and she pulled her coat tighter around her.

Cowering deep inside her scarf, she summoned her courage.

The window was only a few steps away.

The glass was steamed up and Bea hesitated, torn between fear and curiosity. But her feet were getting colder and colder doing nothing. She needed to make up her mind.

She rubbed the windowpane with her glove and saw Santa Claus bopping inside to the music.

She could hardly believe her eyes.

It was enough of a shock to discover her neighbour was Santa Claus, but to see him like this,

a man of his age playing the air guitar and dancing like a teenager, was just amazing!

A few seconds later, Santa Claus switched off the stereo, picked out a book from the bookcase and settled into his armchair to read.

Bea was pleased to see him so absorbed in his book, sipping peacefully on a cup of tea and stoking the fire as he turned the pages. Much more like Santa Claus.

Her heart was still racing when she got home.

Isn't life strange?

When you're least expecting something, that's when it comes along and surprises you.

Bea was all grown up now and had ended up

living right next door to her hero, Santa Claus!

You must be wondering why Bea didn't approach Santa as soon as she discovered he was her neighbour? Why didn't she go and knock on Santa's door after all the letters she'd written to him over the years?

The answer's easy: she was too shy!

If Santa had chosen not to reply to all her letters, there must be a reason.

Looking back, she realized they had been a bit soppy and if she were to speak to him now, in person, it would be far too embarrassing.

She'd faint with nerves before she ever managed to ring the bell!

12

Meanwhile, Santa was pushing ahead determinedly with his search for a job.

Going back to the newspaper again, he spotted:

> Call-centre staff wanted.

'Hmmm . . .' he mumbled.

> Requirements:
> Able to work flexible hours.

'Ah! My schedule couldn't be more flexible,' he exclaimed, laughing.

> Looking for highly driven,
> diligent individuals.

'Excellent! In my long and honourable career, I've never missed a delivery,' he said proudly.

Santa jumped to his feet, hurriedly grabbed the reins, fired up Dasher and Dancer and set off once more, his spirits higher than ever despite his recent setbacks.

Bea saw him leave his house for the third time that week. This was highly unusual – she'd learned very quickly that Santa was a bit of a lazybones – and she was growing increasingly concerned.

'What on earth is going on . . . ?' she mumbled
to herself, worried.

Santa strode into the call centre and looked around
warily, sizing the place up.

*Let's hope they won't have a problem with my long
white beard.*

Or want me to be dynamic.

Or make a song and dance about my age.

All these things were buzzing around Santa's head when the manager came over to shake his hand.

'Welcome aboard, my dear Santa Claus. Let me show you to your booth. It's a bit tight, but . . .'

He'd given Santa the job in less than a blink of an eye!

Santa Claus was shown into an enormous room with more than one hundred call handlers squeezed into tiny booths, each staring at a computer screen.

Exciting, he thought.

But it was also a little odd: the manager hadn't asked if he knew how to use a computer. And he hadn't given Santa any instructions on what he was supposed to be doing.

The excitement quickly wore off.

That's when Santa noticed the manager was shaking hands with everyone who came through the door, summoning them in with a: 'Welcome aboard!'

What he didn't say was how much they'd be earning.

Now, Santa Claus wasn't one to dwell on money, but he did have his pride.

He leaned over to a young man with the spiky hair in the next booth and asked, 'What am I supposed to do?'

'Call up a random person and . . .'

Santa grinned. 'And tell them a joke!'

'No, no jokes! You have to convince the person on the other end of the phone to buy a vacuum cleaner.'

'But what if they don't want a vacuum cleaner?'

'It's your job to convince them they do. Whatever it takes!'

Santa Claus didn't like the sound of that 'whatever it takes'. Not one little bit.

'But—'

'But what?' the manager interrupted, popping out from behind Santa. He obviously wasn't used to being contradicted.

'But . . . I've spent my entire life taking children the things they've always dreamed of . . .'

'And?'

'Dreams are important . . .'

'And?'

'I can't force someone to want something. And if

they don't want it there's no way I could convince them to buy it.'

'Well, these are the rules. If you don't like them, you know where the door is!'

The manager was so rude that Santa did just what he suggested. He turned and headed for the

door, his tummy sending computers tumbling in all directions as he stormed past them, wreaking havoc all the way to the exit.

13

'I'll try one more job and that's it,' Santa Claus said to himself, now very exasperated.

He passed the barber's shop again on his way home.

He pulled the reindeer over.

'Maybe I should just . . .'

Yes, his mind was made up. It was time for a change. And that change would start right here at the barber's.

Something caught Santa's attention as he went to open the door.

There was a large sheet of white paper sticking to the shop window.

'Aha!' Santa Claus twirled his beard. 'Now, what could this be about?' he wondered to himself.

It was a public notice.

The local council was recruiting ten new binmen.

'A binman?'

Santa had never thought about it before, but he

was definitely cut out for public service!

Come to think of it, he'd make a great traffic warden, too. After all, he was very good at leaving surprises for people and appearing out of nowhere when they least expected it. But he was also too nice – he'd never be able to serve a penalty on someone or divert the traffic. He'd much rather wave 'hello' to everyone.

Maybe he'd make a better fireman. He had the red suit already!

'But a binman, now there's an idea!' he pondered out loud.

It didn't take long to make up his mind. The very next day, Santa Claus handed in an application to the local council office.

85

14

A few days later, Santa Claus received a reply. He was overjoyed to read that he had passed the selection criteria. He met all the requirements, the letter said, and they were therefore pleased to offer him a job.

'Hooray!' Santa cheered.

Santa Claus was going to collect people's recycling.

They gave him a big white truck with a flashing yellow light on the roof. He loved driving it.

Best of all, Santa was doing something useful, and at night, when no one could see him.

He collected plastic on Mondays, glass on Tuesdays, metal on Wednesdays, paper on Thursdays, food waste on Fridays and rested on Saturdays and Sundays.

In his new position he'd also bumped into an old friend, Winnie, who'd also been forced to go out and find a second job. Just like him, her seasonal work delivering sweets at Halloween was no longer enough to last the rest of the year.

Santa's friend always had holes in her shoes. He didn't know if it was out of habit or because she couldn't be bothered to get new ones. It didn't matter, though, because her job was now to zip around the city sweeping the streets with her big broom. She did it so quickly that her workmates would always say, 'You go so fast anyone would think you were flying on that broom!'

*

Santa Claus worked long hours.

At ten o'clock at night he'd punch his timecard at the big warehouse and climb into his truck.

He emptied all the bins in the city centre before heading out to the suburbs. At first light, he'd empty the last one outside his own house. Can you guess which one was second last?

Yes, it was Bea's. Bea, who'd once been completely unaware that Santa Claus was her neighbour, now had no idea he was her new binman.

15

Back at the International Postal Service, things were utter mayhem. Christmas was fast approaching and the Super Director was shaking up the place like a bottle of ketchup.

Before the workers had time to blink, he had passed a new rule saying that all Christmas presents would be delivered by drones and announced to the world on live TV that not only were Santa's helpers being cut, but that Santa Claus had been let go, too!

Santa Claus's worst nightmare had just come true – they really were firing him – but he wasn't doing too badly: he liked his second job as much

as his first one. And just as well, because it was the only one he'd been able to get. He was no longer a seasonal worker and the eleven months' holiday he'd once enjoyed were nothing more than a distant memory.

Each new day at the postal depot brought fresh havoc as the Super Director introduced one major shake-up after another. His newest announcement was that everything was to be digitized.

Handwritten letters would disappear. Gone forever!

Instead, wish lists would be sent with a click to an enormous digital folder called the Christmas Inbox.

It was time to say goodbye to the paper archive!

All the 'fanciful' and 'impossible' letters (codes F01 and F02) that hadn't gone into the cauldron were to be returned to sender, meaning that all the

idealists and the dreamers would get their letters back, maybe years after they'd written them. There were thousands of them! It was a cruel, heartless decision, but the Super Director would not be budged on it.

The twenty-fifth of December came and went, and Santa Claus had been a binman for three weeks.

The more he lugged sacks of rubbish around on his back, the more he realized his second job was very similar to his first one.

The only difference was where he took the sacks (to the recycling plant instead of to children) and what was in them (no gifts, only plastic, paper, glass.)

Then one starry, starry night, he had an idea.

Most games are made of plastic, aren't they? he thought to himself. *I could turn all these plastic bottles I collect into toy boats, or trucks or cars, and the bottle tops could be wheels. Who knows how many different toys could be made out of the paper and cardboard!*

He set to work straight away. As soon as he got home at dawn he rang his friend Winnie – the one with the broom and the holey shoes whom people at work had been raving about because she was so fast and so creative.

'Dear Winnie, you've become a bit of a star in this industry. I have a proposal for you!'

'What's it about?'

'Why don't we go back to our real jobs: delivering presents.'

'That's impossible!'

'Nothing's impossible,' Santa Claus

declared. 'Here's the plan: we'll continue emptying bins, but instead of throwing the rubbish away we'll turn it into toys.'

'Hmm . . .' Winnie considered Santa's idea. 'Yes, it might work, but the Super Director at the International Postal Service will never go along with it.'

'I know, so that's why we'll bypass him. We'll do it ourselves. We'll join forces and form a co-operative!' Santa gushed, bursting with excitement.

'My dear friend, these are tough times.'

'I know, I know, but we if work together and dare to dream . . .'

Winnie wasn't sure, but finally accepted.

'Go on, then. We may be old, but there's plenty of life left in us, for sure!'

16

Quicker than a wink, the co-operative was signed and sealed. Santa Claus and Winnie were going it alone. They'd gather paper, plastic, glass and aluminium during the year, and turn them into toys.

When December came round the following year and the festive season began, they would ask children to send letters to them instead, and Santa and Winnie would make toys and grant wishes for all of them.

True to tradition, Santa would deliver the presents with his reindeer on Christmas Eve.

Winnie, on the other hand, would deliver her presents just like she used to, at Halloween, flying from house to house on her broom, wearing her holey shoes. She flatly refused to get a new pair. Not even fashionable ones with heels!

Now, the co-operative was just the two of them and two people couldn't get gifts to every child in every part of the world. Not right away, anyway. But, over time, the pair planned to extend their reach and return to the present-delivering heights of their heyday.

They would employ ten helpers, then ten more, until they reached one hundred. Children's hopes and dreams would be rekindled and the Super Director of the International Postal Service would be forced to take notice of the 'stuffy old traditionalists', as he'd disparagingly called them when he saw them come back on the scene with their modern methods and original ideas.

All this would happen later, though Santa Claus didn't know it yet.

17

The months rolled by and, as Santa and Winnie worked hard collecting rubbish and turning it into presents, the International Postal Service finished returning to sender all the letters that contained requests classed as fanciful and impossible.

One morning, Bea heard a knock at the door.

'Who could that be?' she wondered, feeling a little worried.

Through the spyhole, she saw a young man wearing a hat and a blue suit, holding a package.

Curiosity getting the better of her, she opened the door.

'Good morning. These are for you.' The postman held out the package. 'They were sent to your old address, but the new tenants told me where to find you.'

Taken aback, Bea accepted the package and shut the door, not saying a word.

She opened it.

She was even more stunned when she recognized her letters, her handwriting, her old address, the envelopes and the stamps she had so carefully stuck on to them.

Several tears tumbled onto the pile of yellowed paper.

Bea realized her letters had never reached their destination. On impulse, she stuffed them all back in the package and tossed the whole lot in the bin.

18

That same evening, Santa Claus did his usual rounds. It was paper-collection day.

It was December now, and bitterly cold.

On emptying Bea's bin, he noticed something strange.

Curious, he peeked inside.

Families often threw away old memories – photos, school jotters, diaries, books – but this enormous bundle of letters looked interesting.

He looked closer, and got quite a shock when he saw who they were addressed to. In fact, he could hardly believe his eyes!

He rushed home, put on his slippers and sat down in his armchair. With the bundle on his knee, he began to read, many years later than he should have:

Dear Santa Claus, you have the best job

in the world! I think you're amazing!

Do you like going out on a bike?

What are your hobbies?

What do you do when it's not Christmas?

Can you teach me to fly?

Are you ticklish?

Do you like candyfloss?

I'd love to go out on your sleigh and

visit every country in the world,

the hot ones and the cold ones.

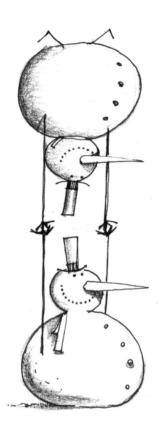

19

The year was drawing to an end and business was booming at the co-operative. They received more and more letters and had a full schedule for Christmas.

But Santa Claus's mind kept going back to Bea's letters. It hadn't been his fault that he'd never written back to her: no one had given them to him and he wasn't allowed to reply anyway. Still, he felt he should do something.

He became forgetful and clumsy at work.

He lost his appetite and his beard became thinner.

The reindeer were worried about him.

A few days later, he opened a drawer in the bathroom he hadn't opened for years.

It contained a razor and a can of shaving foam.

What a mess he made. He stuck tiny pieces of toilet paper to all the cuts on his skin. Oh, how his

skin tingled. But he rinsed his face, put on some arctic raspberry aftershave . . . and got the surprise of his life!

He looked a lot younger.

In fact, he was unrecognizable. Even he had to look twice at the face in the mirror.

He switched on the oven, opened the fridge and did what he did best – better than delivering gifts, recycling rubbish, dancing to rock music and reading books – he made a delicious apple cake with cream and a pinch of cinnamon.

While the cake was still piping hot and smelling delicious, he packed it up and went into the garage with it to get his reindeer. Then he changed his mind.

'No! I'll walk today!'

Bubbling with nerves, Santa slowly covered the short distance to Bea's house. He'd dressed carefully

for the occasion. Gone was the well-known red suit, which had been replaced by a pair of formal trousers and smart shoes. Oh, and a red jumper (it was his favourite colour, after all).

By the time he reached Bea's house, he was out of breath.

'I'll start back at the gym tomorrow!' he promised himself. 'It'll make me even more efficient at work!'

He rested for a couple of minutes then walked the last few metres.

20

Santa was unrecognizable, dressed so smartly and with no beard.

And Santa Claus had never seen Bea. From the dates on her letters, he'd worked out her age. She had to be nearly as advanced in her years as him.

Would she open the door to him?

Standing with his finger on the bell, Santa Claus patted himself down one last time. Then he pressed it.

What a surprise Bea will get when she opens the door! he thought.

*

Bea had presumed it would be the postman, back with another bundle of letters she'd sent years ago.

Why bother answering the door? she thought.

But the bell kept ringing. Once, twice, three, then four times.

She edged closer to the door. It wasn't the postman – it was a smartly-dressed man with a clean-shaven face.

Hmm, who can it be? she thought.

'Who's there?' she asked, without opening the door.

'Hello. It's your neighbour . . .'

'I don't have any neighbours.'

'I live not far from here, in the last house before the mountains and the long sheet of ice.'

'That's impossible. Someone else lives there.'

'But that's me.'

'No, no, a man with a beard lives there.'

'I cut it off.'

'That man wears a red suit.'

'I got changed.'

Bea didn't know what to do. Could this man on her doorstep really be Santa Claus? He didn't look a bit like him.

'Dearest Bea, will you open the door? I have a cake for you and it's getting cold.'

Bea was rooted to the spot behind the door.

Then Santa blurted, 'I have your letters.'

Bea jumped. Her hands trembled.

Santa Claus took a deep sigh. 'I'm a binman by night. I found them in your rubbish. No one ever gave them to me. If only I'd got them, I would've replied. Honestly . . .'

Santa heard a timid click. The door opened.

His eyes met those of an elderly woman with

greying hair, but whose eyes shone as bright as a child's.

Bea invited Santa Claus inside, took his coat and showed him into the living room.

They cut the cake and ate a slice together in silence.

It was still warm.

21

It was icy cold out that evening, but the pair went into Bea's garden to look at the sky.

It wasn't snowing and there were no clouds.

The stars above seemed to go on forever on a blanket of swirling, twirling, multicoloured light.

'How beautiful!' they whispered in unison.

Gazing up at the northern lights, Santa Claus and Bea embraced and, in perfect unison, said, 'I think the dreams of children everywhere will come true tonight.'

It was the night before Christmas.

About the Author

Michele D'Ignazio was born in Cosenza, Southern Italy. He is the author of Italian bestseller *Story of a Pencil* and its two sequels. Very active in promoting reading in young people, when not writing, Michele tours bookshops and schools in Italy meeting thousands of young readers. *Il Secondo Lavoro di Babbo Natale* is a bestseller in Italy and has now sold in six languages worldwide.

About the Illustrator

Sergio Olivetti is an architect, graphic designer, teacher, illustrator and author of children's books. He lives in Italy and has published many different children's books with Rizzoli, Sinnos, Bacchilega and more.

About the Translator

Denise Muir has published a variety of translated works for children of all ages, including Manuela Salvi's *Girl Detached*, *Red Stars* by Davide Morosinotto and *The Distance Between Me and the Cherry Tree* by Paola Peretti which was nominated for the CILIP Carnegie Medal 2019 and the IBBY Honour List 2020.